Franny's Fable

Heather Harrison

This is a work of fiction. Names, characters, places, and incidents are products of the author's imagination or are used fictitiously and are not to be construed as real. Any resemblance to actual events, locations, organizations, or persons, living or dead, is entirely coincidental.

World Castle Publishing, LLC
Pensacola, Florida
Copyright © Heather Harrison 2018
Paperback ISBN: 9798891264069
eBook ISBN: 9781629898667
First Edition World Castle Publishing, LLC, January 29, 2018
http://www.worldcastlepublishing.com

Licensing Notes

Cover: Karen Fuller
Editor: Maxine Bringenberg

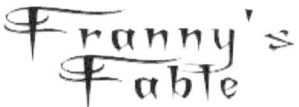

Between smears of soapy glass, Franny McClain stared at her reflection. A dark curtain of night clung to the other side of the window, depicting a replica of the brightly lit kitchen behind her.

Her eyes, golden brown and dull, lay protuberant under thin, translucent lids. Her face appeared lived in, a valley of sagging skin, pale and blemished with age, holding the story of decades passed. Water ran over her waxy hands while rivulets of blood washed down the drain, her sins tunneling their way through the frozen earth.

Trembling hands dropped the knife and it landed in the sink. Franny stared at the blade. Grabbing the damp washcloth from beside the sink, she covered her face, muffling screams. Tears poured relentlessly down her cheeks and seeped beyond the rag, leaving wet trails down her neck.

When she could cry no more, she threw the rag down, finished her chores, and turned off the light. Waddling slightly, Franny headed to the library. She ignored the piles of books haphazardly stacked upon the shelves, searching behind her husband's desk instead. In the oak-laden cabinets she found a bottle of twenty-year-old Scotch and a pair of crystal tumblers. In the bottom drawer, behind a thick stack of files, she located a pack of Pall Malls and matches. It had been over thirty years since she'd quit smoking, but every five years or so she would buy a pack, stare at it awhile to see if it still had a hold on her, and then store it away. Tonight, she had no intention of staring at the pack. She was going to smoke the whole damn thing.

She lit a match, pausing before bringing the flame to the tip of the cigarette. A soft scratching sound reached her ears, and although she knew it was only the wind brushing the snow-laden trees against the house, she leaned back in the chair, glancing into the bedroom. Silhouetted against the blue-hued light pouring through the window was her husband's body. Franny nervously watched for the smallest of movements, but he remained still. A solitary flame from the match traveled down the stem, and she muttered a curse as it burned the tips of her fingers. Casting the match down, she lit another, this time waving it out after billows of smoke came from the end of the cigarette.

She turned on the computer and poured herself a full glass of Scotch. Soon she would have to face her consequences, but tonight was hers. Tonight she would tell her story. She drank her Scotch, staring at the blank computer screen, while her husband lay on a piece of tarp draped across the bed, his waxy eyes staring at the ceiling, blood seeping from an open wound. A cramping, burning ache seized her body. She took deep breaths, bending over until the pain passed. When it did, Franny set her glass down and began to type. *The year was nineteen sixty-six, and I was twenty-two and beautiful....*

It was at the height of the feminist movement when my friends and I, all newly graduated college students, decided to travel the world. For two years the four of us scrounged and saved to afford the trip. My parents didn't have much money, so I never bothered to ask them for help, but was pleasantly surprised when my grandparents gave me enough to travel comfortably as a graduation gift. Years later I discovered my grandfather had been against the idea, but my grandmother, who I am affectionately named after, convinced him to give it to me. Married at fifteen and a mother of seven, she had never gotten a chance to see the world, and sometimes, over a cup of tea, I would detect regret in her eyes.

Our first stop was to be three weeks in Paris, France. I still remember the thrill of that plane ride, the feeling of awe when looking out the window.

Rebekah sat beside me. Out of the four of us, we were the closest. Like me, she wanted something more than being a teacher or homemaker like many of the girls our age aspired to be. Jeanette and Bobbie, our other two friends, were both drama majors and about as opposite as you could get. Jeanette was tall, slim, with a love for romance and comedies. Bobbie was short, nearly pixie-like, and soft spoken.

It was our second day in Paris when I met him. My feet ached from touring the tower and other historical landmarks, but we continued until late evening. Two hours before nightfall, we stopped at a bar that, according to a few of the locals, served some of the best cuisine. Tired and thirsty, we grabbed a table at the back.

I was halfway through my meal when Rebekah elbowed me in the side and whispered, "That guy over there keeps staring at you."

I looked up.

A pair of cold gray eyes met mine, the

intensity radiating from the man behind them making me shiver. I quickly looked away, but that first glance at his face would be forever etched in my memory. A thin, sloping nose and small set eyes were a stern contrast to his chiseled cheekbones and the soft groove above his upper lip. He was exquisite, yet from that single look I got the impression that most people would not be able to pick him out of a crowd. He seemed to fade into the darkness.

For the next ten minutes I slowly ate my dinner, peering up occasionally to see him still staring at me. Rebekah informed our other two friends, who kept cutting their eyes between the two of us and snickering behind their hands.

"I wish he would quit staring," I mumbled.

"Go say something to him then," Jeanette whispered. "When have you ever cowed down for a man?"

I rolled my eyes. Jeanette was an active member of the feminist group at our college.

Thankfully, Bobbie spoke up. "No way, that's dangerous. That guy could be a total

psycho."

The rest of us nodded our heads. It wasn't until after the third mixed drink that I changed my mind. Feeling sure of myself, I sashayed over to his table, pulled out a chair, and sat down across from him. He held a glass to his lips. I tried to play it cool while he took a considerable amount of time draining the amber liquid. After what seemed like an eternity, he set the glass down with a thud.

Now that I was up close, the air about him seemed to crackle with electricity. Those intense gray eyes piercing through me seemed mildly annoyed. It took me a moment to find my voice.

"I'm Franny."

He didn't respond. Instead, he leaned back in the wooden chair, his eyes roaming over my body.

Fine then. Two can play at this game.

I reached forward and pulled out a cigarette from the pack he had sitting on the table. I didn't recognize the brand, but I did recognize the pack of matches sitting on the top. They were from a diner we had passed by a few blocks back. I lit the cigarette and leaned back, mimicking his body language.

"And you are?" I asked between puffs of smoke.

"Not interested," he replied, his voice sensual yet full of gravel.

He held his hand out and I started to reach for it, thinking he wanted to shake mine, but then he snapped his fingers and pointed to the matches I held. Irritated with his attitude and flustered with the way he made my heart race, I pulled my hand away and stood.

"No, I think I'm going to keep them, Mister Not Interested. Have a nice night."

I turned and walked away, but not before I saw the corner of his mouth twitch upward.

By the time I finished whispering to the girls about what happened and looked up, his seat was empty. That was the first time I ached for him, but nowhere close to the last.

The next few days were spent hiking

and touring the underground. Having been born and raised in small suburbia, I'd never witnessed beauty like I did in France. I found myself gaping like a small child who'd just experienced their first snow. Luckily, I wasn't the only one. Out of the four of us, only Jeanette had traveled outside the state, and she hadn't been farther than Florida. But between the awe and exhaustion, my mind kept traveling back to the man from the other night. I didn't understand why I couldn't let the memory go, why a man I'd only briefly met had such a hold on me. When I laid down to sleep, I found myself cradling the set of matches I'd stolen, fantasizing about having his hands all over me. I tried to tell myself I only wanted to tell him off, but I knew in my heart I was denying the truth…I wanted the man like I'd never wanted anyone before.

On the fifth morning I suggested we have breakfast at the diner whose name was written across the matchbook. The girls all nodded, except Rebekah, who raised her eyebrows and gave me a slight smile.

Like I said, she knew me and knew me well.

I spent an inordinate amount of time getting ready that morning. The fitted, short, pink dress I wore, belted around the waist, and gold sandals made me feel like a woman. I remember looking in the mirror and thinking I looked like Audrey Hepburn. My friends yelled impatiently, so I grabbed the pack of matches and we walked to the diner.

When the door opened, I was surprised to see so many people packed into the metal rimmed booths. Underneath the loud clamor of patrons, I heard soft music playing. The place was small and dimly lit, which made me wonder about the cleanliness of it. The smell, though, was delectable, and my stomach began to rumble. My friends and I slid into one of the few empty booths and began to scan the menu. Every few seconds I would glance up when the bell chimed to see who'd entered.

Rebekah leaned over and whispered in my ear, "You're looking for him, aren't you?"

I gave her a cross look out of the corner of my eye, but didn't answer. She tapped me on the shoulder and pointed toward the counter. It took me a moment to realize what she was pointing at, but when I did, my eyes were immediately drawn to him. He was behind the window, handing out orders to the waitresses. He suddenly stopped his work and glanced at me.

In the light of day his face looked softer, sweeter somehow, but when our eyes met, his jaw clenched and his eyes became slits. Hurt and insulted, I quickly looked away. Jeanette and Bobbie were too engrossed in their menu to have noticed, but Rebekah saw me blinking back tears. I heard her mouth the word "Asshole" and nodded my head in agreement.

The waitress, an elderly woman with dirty nails, came over to take our order, giving me a much-needed distraction. When I glanced back over at him he was busy cooking, and paid me no mind. I listened to the conversation about the day's plan, but pretended to be too busy

15

eating my meal to comment. I needed time to think. I was mad, pissed really, but more than anything, I was hurt. I'd never felt such contempt from someone whose name I didn't even know.

When the waitress came back with our checks, I asked, "Ma'am, what's the cook's name? I'd like to thank him for such a good meal."

The lady frowned and shook her head. "Name's Jamie, but don't bother thanking him. He's not the most pleasant of people." She tore a sheet off the notepad and handed it to me.

I took it, ignoring my friends as they crooned their heads around to get a look at the man behind the counter, and said, "It's pretty busy today. You must be exhausted. What time do you usually get off?" I paused, checking out her name badge before adding, "Evelyn?"

"I'm here until close."

I pretended to be appalled. "That's horrible."

"Well, we close at six, but that's still long enough."

Her attention shifted as another table whistled, waving her down. She sighed and narrowed her eyes.

"Well, Evelyn, I hope the rest of your day gets better."

Nodding, the woman turned and walked very slowly over to the table that was waving to her.

As soon as she was out of hearing range, Bobbie chipped in, "That's the guy from the bar, isn't it?"

I smiled and nodded, a plan already forming. There was no way I was going to let him treat me like crap, at least not until he got to know me.

Jeanette giggled behind her hands, commenting, "You came here on purpose! You're up to something, aren't you?"

Both Jeanette and Bobbie were excited by the idea of me smoozing on some guy, but Rebekah, the only one who had seen the hatred on his face, shook her head.

"Don't. I don't like him."

I ignored her and said, "Let's go pay and get out of here."

While I approached the register and waited for the other girls to pay, I kept my eyes on Jamie. He never looked up, but I could tell he was aware of my presence by the way he pointedly avoided looking in my direction, all the while frowning. The man behind the cash register took the slip out of my hand and rang me up, his eyes sliding between me and Jamie, who I refused to stop staring at.

I took my receipt, and as I passed by the food window, I yelled, "See ya' later, Jamie!"

This time he did raise his head, a look of surprise on his face.

I smirked and walked out.

Nothing makes you feel more empowered than a group of girls conspiring with you against a man. By early afternoon we had devised at least five different plans to entice Jamie into liking me. Because of his smartass attitude, most of them involved me breaking his heart in the end.

When Jeanette and Bobbie busied themselves trying on clothes at one of the local shops, Rebekah pulled me aside.

"It's fun talking about this, but you're not really going to go through with it, are you?"

Honestly, at that moment, I was on the fence. Most likely, if it hadn't been for the way Rebekah stood with her hands on her hips, or the I-know-better-than-you look on her face, I probably would have chickened out. I'm nothing if not a fighter.

"Of course I am," I said, turning my back to her, pretending to look at some bracelets. "It's not like he's some homeless guy. We know where he works. He's just a run of the mill asshole."

"If that's true, why are you so obsessed with him?"

I turned towards her and leaned against the counter, dramatically fanning my face. "What I meant was, hot, sexy, run-of-the-mill asshole."

Rebekah tried to keep a straight face, but

her mouth started twitching and a few seconds later, we doubled over laughing. When the other girls came around they gave us strange looks, but we were too deep in our fit to explain.

Purchases in tow, we made our way back to the hotel. Five-thirty rolled around, and I wasn't sure if my nerves were going to allow me to get out the door or have me running to the bathroom. In the end, a few shots of French whiskey and some hurrahs from the girls helped my self-confidence and got me out the door.

It was still light outside when I arrived at the diner. I walked an extra block around so I wouldn't pass by the window, on the offhand chance he might see me and run out the back. I picked a shaded spot between the diner and alleyway where I could stand unnoticed. After ten minutes the door opened and Evelyn stepped out. I turned away and pretended to window shop at the bakery next door. Digging in her purse, she pulled out a smoke, lighting it before trudging off in the other direction.

Twenty minutes passed, and I was beginning to doubt Jamie worked until close when he stepped out onto the sidewalk. He wore blue jeans and a button-down shirt, sleeves rolled above the elbow. The sight of him made my heart pound erratically. He turned his head, looking towards the east. I took a deep breath and leaned against the wooden post, waiting to see if he would notice.

When he glanced toward me his gaze met mine, and before he had a chance to gather himself, I saw it in his eyes. Even at a distance I could sense his lust for me. His lips parted slightly and his eyes widened, the pupils swelling until the gray was almost black. He took two steps in my direction before stopping, his eyes turning sharp.

"What are you doing here?"

I raised my eyebrows and dug in my bag, pulling out a cigarette and his matches. Taking my time, as he had the other night, I lit the smoke and strolled over, holding out his matchbook. He took several steps back, and for a second I thought he was going to take off running, but he seemed to gain control, the glare returning to his face.

"I told you I would see you later. Plus, I thought I'd better return your matches before your vendetta against me got any worse."

He glanced at the matches. His right hand twitched upward slightly and then dropped back down to his side.

"You keep them."

He turned and started to walk away. Luckily, I'd been expecting that. He was faster than me, but I still managed to catch up without tripping or losing my composure.

"Thanks," I said, slipping the matches into my purse. "I'm the world's worst at losing these things. It always helps to have extra. I'm from America, by the way. Nebraska, to be exact. Did you grow up in France?"

His eyes shifted to me. I could tell I'd caught him off guard. He opened his mouth to speak, but then snapped it shut, picking up speed. I ran to keep up with him, thankful I'd spent the last two years on the track team.

"It doesn't seem like you have a French accent, so I'm guessing you're from abroad. You can correct me if I'm wrong."

He squeezed his eyes shut and his lips became a thin line.

I continued. "Anyway, my friends and I are traveling the country. We graduated from college last month. I have a degree in history, specifically European history. Eventually, I plan on getting my masters and becoming a museum curator."

I wondered if he had gone to college and thought about asking him, but decided against it. He seemed to be a few years older than me, and considering his job, the question might be offensive. Plus, he still looked like he was ready to bite my head off.

"Oh, you'll need to take a left on this next road."

That stopped him in his tracks. He turned to me, a look of confusion on his face as he asked, "Why?"

"So you can walk me home," I responded, flicking the cigarette to the ground. "My hotel's that way."

"No."

"Of course you are."

"No."

He began walking again, taking long strides in the opposite direction. I tagged along.

"Where are we going then?" I asked.

"*We* are going nowhere."

At least he's talking now.

I wasn't sure of my next move. The only thing I did know was he seemed less angry than confused now. I considered that a good sign.

"You know, it's rude to make a lady walk herself home, especially when it's getting close to nightfall."

"I don't care."

I couldn't tell if he meant that or not, but I decided to push my luck.

"I could get hurt or lost. I don't think you want that to happen to me. Plus, I'm nearly positive you want to walk me home. You enjoy my company."

I had never seen someone so exasperated with me. Jamie stopped mid-stride, his mouth hanging open. He shook his head and ran his hands through his deep brown hair, pulling at it. His nostrils flared slightly, and I was suddenly glad we weren't the only two people on the street.

"Franny, I am not walking you to your hotel. Go home."

I don't know what reaction he expected from me, but it probably wasn't the one he got. I smiled. Hell, I couldn't help myself...I positively beamed.

"You remembered my name."

Maybe it was the ridiculousness of my statement or just the grin on my face, but the side of his mouth turned up and he started laughing. It was a sweet sound, deep but musical at the same time. I waited until he was done before speaking again.

"So, does that mean you've changed your mind?"

Jamie shook his head, the grin gone but the light still in his eyes.

"No, but they might."

He pointed to a crowd across the street. I scanned the area, thinking he had seen my friends. When I couldn't find them I spun back around to ask who he was talking about, but he was gone.

Well, shit.

We all stayed up late that night, debating the story behind Jamie's attitude. The ideas ranged from shy, bullied kid, to serial killer, hunted by the law. I listened and giggled with the rest, but spent most of the night thinking about what to do when I saw him again.

The next morning my friends wanted to eat at a fancy restaurant. None of them seemed shocked when I told them I was going back to the diner and would meet up with them later. The morning was brisk and my heels clicked on the sidewalk, echoing down the empty street. I wanted to get to the diner early so I could get a seat at the bar.

The moment I stepped in the door, he knew. Whether he had seen me through the window or just sensed me, I don't know. I never asked, but I think it was the latter. Jamie gave me a curt nod as if he'd been expecting me, and then went back to work. His acknowledgment wasn't the least bit friendly, but it wasn't angry either.

I ordered some crepes, greeting Evelyn like we were old friends, and watched Jamie behind the grill. No wonder the place was so busy; he was a master in the kitchen. Every once in a while I would catch him watching me out of the corner of his eye and I would smile. When I did, his jaw would clench.

I finished my meal and paid for it, yelling, "See ya later, Jamie."

Without looking up, he shook his head.

Too bad I wasn't asking permission.

Apparently, I wasn't the only one on a romantic streak. Jeanette had been flirting around with one of the waiters at breakfast, and they made plans to meet up with him and a few of his friends at a bar. I wasn't crazy about the idea, especially since Jeanette mentioned it might be a good idea for me to "Meet some other guys besides the weirdo at the diner," but I didn't want to let my friends down, so I agreed. Of course, that wasn't going to stop me from meeting with Jamie.

I left the hotel at five and brought a book with me. Settling down outside the diner, with the book in my lap, I didn't have to wait long before Jamie came out. Just as I expected, he was trying to leave early to avoid me. He saw me, took an irritated breath, shook his head, and started walking away. I hopped up and followed him.

"So where did you learn to cook? I was watching you today. I don't know why you work at this diner. You can have a job in any of the restaurants around here."

"I don't want a job at another restaurant."

I wasn't sure, but I thought that was the

longest sentence he had said to me yet. That gave me hope.

"Where are you from, anyway? You never told me last night."

"Everywhere. I move around a lot."

Although he was looking straight ahead, I had the feeling he was more aware of me than he let on. He wore a light jacket that smelled faintly of leather, his hands shoved deep in the pockets.

"That explains the lack of accent. How old are you?" I asked.

"Twenty-seven."

"See, that wasn't so hard. So far I know your name, your age, and that you move around a lot. By this time next week, we might be friends."

Jamie frowned, an overwhelming sadness filling his gray eyes. Meeting his gaze, I became nervous and missed a step, losing my balance. I felt his hand on my arm, steadying me, his touch sending shivers down the length of my body.

I looked up and said, "Thank you."

He let go of me quickly. After a moment we resumed our walk, but this time I let the silence stretch. The look in his eyes was clear...there was no way he was going to let us be friends or anything else. What bothered me was, I could tell he wanted us to be.

I was lost in my thoughts and didn't notice he had stopped walking until I heard my name slip off his tongue.

"Franny?"

There was a sweetness to the way he said it. Not knowing what he was going to say, I braced myself.

"Yes?"

Jamie nodded to the right. "This is your road."

"Are you offering to walk me home?"

He shook his head.

"That's fine. I'm not going home anyway. Maybe next time then?" I gave him a small smile.

His brow furrowed and he asked, "Where are you going?"

"I promised my friends I would meet them and some guys at a bar."

Maybe I imagined it, but for a second there, I thought he looked upset.

"Well, have a good time then."

I stayed on that street corner, watching him walk away, and even though I didn't follow him, I knew my heart had.

I realized it was the same bar we had gone to on the second night. By the time I got there, Jeanette was hanging on the arm of a tall, muscular guy, while Bobbie seemed engrossed in conversation with a young scholarly type. Truth be told, the last one shocked me. I had suspected (and Rebekah agreed) that Bobbie's tastes were more in the direction of women than men. Neither one of us had ever seen her date. Rebekah was sitting at the table with two guys, one with long blond hair, and the other a dark-haired man wearing yellow-tinted sunglasses.

I joined them and Rebekah lifted an eyebrow. I could tell she was dying to hear about what had happened with Jamie, but I gave an imperceptible shake of my head. Now was not the time.

To my surprise, the guys, who called themselves Jonas and Carol (God bless his parents), could hold an interesting conversation. Both were in music, Jonas working for a recording studio and Carol a bass player for a band called The Clovers, who'd just signed a contract with a minor label. I wasn't interested in either of them, but between the drinks and some intellectual conversation, I was able to suppress my thoughts about Jamie, at least until he walked in the door.

There was no surprise on his face when his eyes landed on me. My breath hitched and my stomach did an uncomfortable flip. I was ecstatic to see him, but felt guilty being there with other guys. For a moment I thought he was going to join us, but he strolled over to the opposite side of the bar, taking a seat in the corner where I could barely see him.

Something was different. His walk seemed

menacing, his steps sharp, posture rigid, fists clenched at his side. The crowd parted for him, and maybe it was my imagination, but I thought they sensed it too.

I leaned over and whispered to Rebekah, "Jamie is here."

Her eyes opened wide and she whispered back, "Did he follow you?"

"I don't think so, but I think he knew I would be here."

Jeanette, a bit drunk, approached the table, arms wrapped around her date, and told us he was going to walk her back to the hotel. Rebekah and I had a hard time not grinning, especially since we knew walking was the last thing on her mind. We were surprised when Bobbie said she wanted to go too, tugging on the arm of her date. That left us with Carol and Jonas, and me with no idea what to do about Jamie.

Rebekah, sensing my dilemma, leaned over and whispered, "Meet me in the bathroom."

She slid out of the booth, making an excuse to the guys. I counted to thirty, preparing my escape, but was thwarted when Jonas slid out of his side of the booth and took Rebekah's spot beside me, placing an arm around my shoulders.

Crap.

I tried to put room between us, but he pulled me in close and said, "I really like you, Franny."

I wish I could say I had some snappy, smart way to put him down, but between the thought of Jamie watching me and my surprise at the turn of events, my mind went blank.

Instead, I said, "Umm…I'm with someone."

His eyes narrowed. "Well, he's not here now, is he?"

That pissed me off. The way he said it let me know he had the obtuse idea I was leading him on, that I was a tease. I started to smart off, but a voice interrupted me.

"Franny?"

Those gray eyes looked past me at Jonas, and I shivered. To this day, I swear Jonas did too.

Rebekah, deciding I wasn't going to meet her, had come back to the table, and seeing the situation, started to stutter, "Jamie, I...uh, I didn't expect to see you here."

"I came to walk Franny home."

He never took his eyes off Jonas, who quickly removed his arm from around my shoulder. Worried this was about to escalate into a fight, I slid out of the booth quickly, grabbing my purse. I muttered goodbye to Rebekah and she nodded. Jamie grabbed me firmly by the arm and steered me towards the door. Before we got there, I glanced back over my shoulder at Rebekah, and the look on her face mirrored my own.

She looked at me like I was about to be eaten by a monster.

Shadows caressed the alleyway, awnings blowing in the night breeze. His shoes were quiet on the cobblestones while mine clicked away, echoing into the night. The silence stretched for half a block before I could take it no longer.

"Where are you taking me?"

"To your hotel."

I could sense his eyes on me, even though I was staring at the ground. With how nervous I was, his statement should have relieved me, but I felt disappointed.

What is wrong with me? Do I really want this stranger, who has done little more than treat me like a nuisance, to take me to his home, to his bed?

I wasn't naïve. I'd had a few relationships in college...two to be exact, both with boys whose inexperience showed in their bedside manner. I had a feeling that would not be a problem with Jamie. Still, that didn't mean I had a death wish. Unfortunately, the part of my brain that was in charge of my sense of self-preservation was weaker than the part that controlled my hormones.

Pull your shit together, Franny.

I sighed.

"Do you want to go back?"

"To the bar?" I asked.

His question confused me. I tilted my head to look at him. In the darkness his eyes seem to shine, but when I blinked, the glow faded away.

"No," I shook my head. "Not at all."

We turned to the left, taking a route I hadn't been down before. A small voice in the back of my head protested, but I shut it out. I had made the choice to stalk him, to trust him, and now, as my momma would say, I needed to lie in the bed I'd made.

"I should thank you, honestly. Jonas was nice, but I'm not interested in *him*."

At this point, there was no reason to play coy. Of course, the drinks I'd had at the bar helped.

Jamie ran his fingers through his hair, pulling a handful toward the back of his crown. It reminded me of how people would wear a rubber band around their wrist and snap it to anytime they thought about doing something bad.

"You're welcome...Franny."

He seemed to taste my name. A measure of chills ran down my spine, making me ache between my legs.

"Tell me more about yourself," he said.

We took another left, and for the first time in my life I felt dull. He wanted to know more about me, and I couldn't come up with a damn thing.

"Like what?"

Another pull at his hair, this time while glancing at the sky as if studying the moon. "Like your favorite color, flower, anything."

"Oh…well, my favorite color is coral, at least for the time being. It tends to change with the day of the week, though. My favorite flower is baby's breath."

"Aren't those just little weeds with white flowers?"

I laughed. It was obvious he wasn't the flower giving type of guy.

"Yes, but they grew in the fields back home, and on Sundays, my momma would braid my hair and weave them in. It always made me feel pretty. What about you?"

"What about me?"

"Favorite color?"

He looked off into the shadows.

"White."

"Why white?"

"Because…it's the opposite of dark."

Huh, I guess I pegged him completely wrong.

"Are you afraid of the dark?" I scoffed at the idea.

He didn't seem to notice. "There's a difference between fear and dislike. I dislike the dark. People are different when they think no one can see them."

"Oh," I said, unsure of how to respond. "What about flowers then?"

Jamie threw his head back, laughing. "No, I don't have any favorite flowers."

The laugh softened his face, but underneath there was still a dangerous quality to it. When he finished, we walked in silence for a bit. I was lost in thought, analyzing his every word, every move, to try and figure out whether he had feelings for me. It was him grabbing me by the hand and pulling me back that got my attention.

"We're here."

I looked up and realized we were standing on the sidewalk in front of my hotel. Then it hit me…I'd never told him where I was staying.

"Have you been stalking me?"

"Me stalking *you*?"

Oh, yeah. Guess he has a point there.

"Do you…um…want to come in for a bit?"

"It's late."

"It's only eight o'clock."

Jamie shook his head.

We were standing about a foot apart, and I wondered, nervously, if he was going to kiss me. My head was tilted back, those sexy eyes staring into mine, and for a brief second, he started to lean in.

There was a noise at the end of the street and a group of gangling teenagers burst around the corner. Jamie leaned back and pulled at his hair again.

"Good night, Franny."

He was a few feet away before I called out to him, "Goodnight, Jamie."

He didn't turn around.

I didn't bother to tell anyone where I was going the next day. I think we were all past that point anyway, since the others also seemed to have fallen under the spell of romance abroad.

Shifting into a booth at the back of the diner, I was sure Jamie hadn't seen me enter. It took me less than three minutes to find out I was wrong.

Evelyn approached, a strange look on her face. She slid a plate in front of me. On it were the crepes I usually ordered, cooked to perfection, and a small sprig of baby's breath.

I spent most of the day wandering around Paris, thinking. Jamie was obviously the secretive type, but that didn't make him bad. At least, that's what I tried to tell myself. Every time I passed by someone with dark hair, I would turn, hoping it was him, knowing it wasn't. At some point, I had to acknowledge the truth…my emotions had gone past lust, and I was drifting toward dangerous waters. I could count the times he'd actually spoken to me on two hands, and yet I was already head over heels in love, fantasizing about marriage and kids.

Cool it, Franny. He lives here and you're leaving soon.

After purchasing a new book I headed to the diner, ten minutes before close. I went inside, nervously taking a seat behind the counter. Evelyn and the elderly gentleman at the cash register both glanced in my direction, but neither bothered to ask me if I wanted anything.

Jamie, who was finishing wiping down the grill, smirked at me before taking off his apron and hanging it up. Without a word he came around the counter, grabbed my hand, and nodded to the others, whose mouths were hanging open. We stepped out into the brightly lit street.

"Are you going to be in trouble for just leaving like that?" I asked.

"I'd better not be," he said, a faint smile teasing his lips. "It's my diner."

"Are you serious? I thought that old man owned it."

Apparently, there was a lot about Jamie I didn't know.

"Most people do. I like to keep it that way."

"Why?"

"I'm sure you've noticed I'm not exactly the social type," he answered, grinning. "Plus, he might as well own it. I cook and pay for everything, but he runs the bills, deals with the customers. I just like to keep busy."

Jamie turned towards my hotel. He was several strides ahead when he realized I'd stopped. Turning around, he tilted his head to the side. The innocence in that gesture, the way he waited for me, filled me with desire.

For some reason, I was reminded of my freshman year in college. I had to recite a poem in front of the class. I shook through the whole thing, my voice warbling, but for the rest of my life, I would never forget the lines of the poem, *The Road Not Taken*, by Robert Frost.

Those final words, *Two roads diverged in a wood, and I...I took the one less traveled by, and that has made all the difference*, popped into my head as I stood at the corner of the street.

"I don't want to go to my hotel."

He raised his brow in question. "Where do you want to go then?"

I gathered all my courage, and even then, my voice trembled when I spoke, "To your place."

Jamie became very still. My head reeled. He wasn't saying no, at least not yet. I took the opportunity and closed the space between us. When I stood a few inches away from him, I touched his chest and felt a tremor run through his body.

"Take me to your place."

"Franny...." His voice was barely a whisper. "I can't."

"Can't or won't?"

He reached up and tugged at his hair again. I realized he didn't know the answer to my question. He wanted me, that was obvious, and I wanted him so bad I thought I would die if he turned me down. I breached the remaining space between us, pressing my body up against his. He returned the favor, putting an arm around me, pulling me close. I could feel him against my belly.

Before I could take it any further, he pulled away.

"No. Go home."

He pushed by me, stomping back towards the diner. I blinked back tears as I watched him leave.

I was hurt and embarrassed. I knew he wanted me, I'd felt the proof. Standing in the middle of the street with my fists clenched, I decided I was tired of playing this game. If there was a reason for him pushing me away, he needed to tell me what it was.

With my mind made up, I waited until he was nearly out of sight before following him home. Three blocks north of the diner, he walked up the steps of a small but quaint house sitting on a corner lot. I wanted to march right up there, force my way in, but I decided it would be best to wait.

In retrospect, there are days when I wish I'd stayed standing in the middle of the street, eventually walking home, nursing a broken heart with my friends and a few strong drinks. How different my life might have been. But I know I would have never found happiness without him.

###

Franny leaned back in the computer chair, snuffing out another cigarette. Her frail body shook with exhaustion and pain, the cramps coming closer together. She stood up stiffly, her joints screaming. The memories were hard. She was wistful for the past and grateful she would never have to live it again. A stack of papers on the desk drew her attention, as they had many times lately. Franny picked them up, ignoring the medical jargon. It all came down to the same thing…Alzheimers. Another wave of pain came, this one much stronger. As it passed, Franny sat down, lighting a cigarette, before continuing her story.

I waited until nine before making my way toward Jamie's home. The girls and I had spent time together, catching up. I lied and told them Jamie had invited me over. I don't know if it was because I was ashamed or if I was already starting to shut the rest of the world out for him. Instead of carrying a purse I carried an overnight bag. In it were my clothes and toothbrush. I wore a long overcoat buttoned down to my knees, and underneath a lacy bra and panty set. Walking down the street, I nervously flitted my eyes left and right, expecting people to point and laugh. I gained a little more confidence in my disguise when no one seemed to notice.

Jamie's yard was slightly overgrown, a few sparse bushes framing the front. I stood there, shaking, holding my bag against my chest.

What if he throws me out?

What if he isn't alone?

The last thought nearly drove me to my knees. If I barged in on him and another woman, it might destroy me. I barely knew him, yet I was drawn to the man in a way I'd never imagined possible.

There was a small light coming from the front window, but it was the only one on in the house. It occurred to me I might be doing this in vain, that he might not be home. Then again, I would never know if I didn't try.

The steps creaked as I climbed them, making me cringe. I didn't want to give him time to think, time to say no. Taking a deep breath, I raised my hand and knocked three times. I heard movement inside, but no one came to the door. I tried again, this time harder. There was no peephole in the door, nor was the window facing where I was standing on the porch. I waited, counting to thirty. I saw a shadow pass beneath the door.

"Jamie?" I whispered.

"Go away, Franny."

His voice was pained, sorrowful.

"Please open the door."

I held my hand against the wood, feeling the paint flake off under my palm. I wished the door would crumble away, removing the distance between us.

"No. I will talk to you tomorrow. Please, just go home."

I didn't have to see him to know he was leaning his head against the door. Why did he put this distance between us? What he was hiding? Whatever it was, he didn't trust me enough to tell me. In my mind, that meant he didn't care.

I didn't hide the hurt in my voice when I spoke, saying, "Please, just for a second. I...I need to see you."

There was a moment of silence, followed by the sound of the latch. The door opened a crack, leaving his face in the shadows.

"Why did you come here, Franny?"

His voice was deeper than I recalled it being. I wished I could see his face clearly, touch him, but he kept to the shadows.

"I...I wanted...."

I stopped, realizing there was nothing I could say to make him let me in. Taking a deep breath, I reached up and began unbuttoning my jacket. When I was down far enough for him to see my pink bra, he opened the door all the way and grabbed my wrist, stopping me.

"What the hell are you doing?"

"Taking my coat off."

His eyes were dark, nostrils flaring. Physically, there were small adaptions in his posture, in the shape of his face, but nothing odd enough to make me question it. It was his attitude that scared me.

When I was a child we owned a dog, a sweet golden lab named Sally. One day, Sally went feral. She chased after me and I climbed a tree, looking down at my sweet pet who was no longer recognizable. That's what Jamie reminded me of.

He saw the fear and let go, a glimpse of the Jamie I knew crossing his face.

"Go home now, Franny." He started to close the door.

I should have done exactly what he said and high-tailed it back to my hotel, but the sadness I saw in his eyes stopped me.

"If you shut that door, I will just take off this jacket and stand on your porch half-naked until you let me in," I threatened.

His eyes widened in disbelief, narrowing when he realized I was telling the truth. "Goddammit, Franny."

He grabbed my wrist and pulled me inside.

The house was sparsely furnished, thick black curtains covering the windows. An aluminum trayed TV dinner with a few pieces of fried chicken sat on a metal tray. There was no television, but a pile of books was stacked beside the beige couch. I only noticed these things because Jamie walked off the moment I stepped inside. I tried to follow after him, but he held a hand out to stop me.

"Give me a moment."

He paced around the living room, tugging at his hair, his free hand clenched into a fist. I was frightened out of my mind, but determined to find out the truth.

"What's wrong with you?" I asked.

Jamie stopped pacing and turned towards me. "It's none of your concern."

God, his voice was deep. The intensity behind his eyes seemed to crackle. I backed up a few steps, surprised when he came toward me.

"The question should be, what is wrong with you, Franny?"

He reached out, his thumb caressing my lips, the rough pad slipping into my mouth, grazing my teeth, and I trembled.

"You're so sweet. You smell like lilac." Leaning in, he ran his nose down the side of my throat, sniffing me. "I bet you taste good too."

I stepped back, my rear end pressing against the wall. Even as I shook in fear, I felt a hot wetness building between my thighs, soaking my panties. He pulled back, his other hand sliding over my jacket, thumping each button along the way. As his hand lowered, he tapped the button that lay directly over the apex of my thighs.

I moaned and he chuckled, an angry, needy sound, murmuring, "You like that, don't you?"

My brain turned into mush. Somewhere deep inside, I knew I should run, knew he was dangerous. I whispered, "I should go."

His face softened, eyes lightening to their regular shade. "Yes, you should."

Neither one of us moved. Nervously I licked my lips. His eyes slid down, watching my tongue slide over the flesh before pulling me forward, his lips greedily pushing against mine. His tongue darted into my mouth, rolling around every inch of it, tasting and sucking. I pressed into him, all thoughts of leaving gone. He pulled back and grabbed the top of my coat, tearing it apart.

"So beautiful."

His eyes, dark again, roamed over my body. He shoved me against the wall, roughly pulling my bra down, exposing my breasts, rolling my nipples between his thumb and forefinger. His mouth left mine, trailing across the collar bones, his lips hot as he suckled my tender rounds. A hand slid between my legs, rubbing the soaked material.

"Baby…," the whisper escaped his lips, "… so wet."

Jamie trailed kisses down my stomach, and I gasped when his tongue ran over my panties, spreading my legs apart as he licked between them. Tiny nibbles grazed my clit, and he opened his mouth wider, sucking at the wet lace. My stomach clenched, muscles tensed, and I felt the first orgasm wash through me. As I moaned and shook, he greedily pushed the panties aside, his tongue darting in and out of my opening, taking my release in his mouth. Lost, euphoric, and slightly drunk on pleasure, I couldn't open my eyes to watch as I heard him removing his clothing. A belt hit the floor, followed by some shuffling. I felt his hands on my shoulders and he turned me around, sliding the rest of my jacket to the floor. He walked me a few steps forward and leaned me over the couch, slipping my panties down to my ankles.

"So exquisite."

I felt his hands trail over my ass, sliding a rough finger over my opening, slipping them in two and three at a time.

He removed his fingers, spreading my cheeks, and trailed them over my hole, rimming it with wetness. I felt a thumb push against the tender area and tried to move away. Jamie held me tightly and pushed firmly, pressing until pain became pleasure. When I moaned he slapped me on the ass, hard. I screamed, my eyes widening in surprise.

"Shhh…," he leaned down and whispered. "I'm going to take you now. Scream like that again and I'll spank you harder next time."

I bit my lips, holding in the next scream as he slapped my ass, his hardness pressing against my opening. He started to push in and

I squirmed, not ready.

"Jamie, no...."

He ignored me, pressing harder, his thick, throbbing cock stretching my flesh, forcing its way inside. The pain was immense and tears ran down my face.

"Relax, Franny. The pain will go away in a second."

Slowly he pulled back, moving back and forth in a gentle motion. He was right, the pain subsided, and replacing it was such pleasure I began to push against him, fighting the rhythm, taking more.

"Oh, Franny...."

He moaned, losing control, and began to move faster, slipping a hand down, rubbing my clit until I felt the explosion coming.

"Harder."

The word slipped from my lips and he pounded into me with such force I gasped for air. The movement stopped and he pushed harder, embedding himself deep within my flesh. I trembled as another climax tore through me, the clenching muscles sucking him deeper. He whispered my name as I felt his warm, thick release fill me.

My legs felt like jelly. Distantly I was aware of him picking me up and carrying me through the house. He knelt on the edge of the bed, gently laying me across the covers. His brow dripping sweat, the eyes lingering on my face had a lost look. Jamie stood over me for a moment before starting to pace, occasionally glancing in my direction at me, shaking his head. I was half-in, half-out, floating on a distant cloud of euphoria.

Somehow, I found my voice and asked, "Are you okay?"

He stopped pacing and said, "No."

I had no clue what could have upset him. Had I done something wrong? He had been rough, admittedly, but instead of being scared, I found myself liking it, craving more. Still, something was not right here.

"Do you want me to leave?" I asked, choking on the words.

"It wouldn't matter if you did."

I frowned, confused. "Why?"

"Because my kind mates for life."

Somehow, I found the strength to sit up, a feeling of dread building within me. "Your kind? You mean family, or is this a religious thing?" I asked hesitantly.

He laughed, the menacing quality coming back. "Neither."

With a wild look in his eyes he came to the bed and sat down in front of me, staring. For a brief second he smiled, a real smile of happiness, but then his face fell and he reached up, tugging at his hair again.

"Why do you do that?"

The euphoria was wearing off, and the little voice in the back of my head was gaining volume, warning me to leave.

He released his hair, letting his hands fall down to the side. "It reminds me to behave."

"Oh."

As awkward and uncomfortable as the conversation was, I still wanted him, needed him. He sat there, lean and muscular, shirtless, with his pants unbuttoned, and I thought he was the sexiest thing I'd ever seen. Before I lost myself to my desire again, I needed to find out what was going on. I reached out, took his hands in mine, and squeezed. He smiled with such love it took my breath away. For a moment I couldn't speak, couldn't move. In the next moment, the smile was gone, replaced by sadness.

Gently, I spoke, "Jamie, what do you mean by your kind? Are you involved in something? Please explain it to me."

The bedsprings squeaked as he stood, again pacing the room. I waited patiently until his voice cut through the gloom.

"I tried to avoid you, Franny, I really did. The first time I saw you, that night in the bar, I knew I wanted you. I'd never felt anything like that before." His head turned, eyes shining in the darkness as he took in my naked form. "You didn't make it easy. You seemed as drawn to me as I was to you. At first I thought maybe you were one, too." Jamie paused before shaking his head and continuing. "No, you were too good, too sweet. I shouldn't blame you. This is all my fault. I could have fought harder, could have left, but I wasn't strong enough, and now...."

His words trailed off, leaving me to ask, "Now what?"

"Now you're mine."

I smiled. "That doesn't sound so bad."

Without warning, he stopped and slammed his fist into the dresser mirror. Shards of glass flew across the room. I screamed.

He leaned down, picking something up off the floor, and came to me, blood pooling around his fist. I scrambled back on the bed, not speaking, my eyes drawn to the large shard of glass in his hands.

He's crazy.

Oh god, I'm going to die.

He lifted the shard of glass, pointing it at me. I flinched and he lowered it. "Please don't be scared. I won't hurt you."

He scrunched his face and I heard a growling

noise emitting from the back of his throat. With his empty hand he began smacking himself on the side of his head. My paralysis broke and I darted to the other side of the room, trying to escape, but he was between me and the door. The noise caught his attention and he stopped, opening his eyes. Slowly he walked towards me.

"I know this is scary for you. Trust me, I'm scared too, but it's too late now. Please, just listen for a second. Can you do that?"

I nodded, my eyes on the piece of glass. Jamie came closer but stopped a few feet away from me. His stance was lowered to where he didn't tower over me, but his eyes were wild, fearful.

"I'm not who you think I am," he said. "No, that's not right. I'm not *what* you think I am. I'm not human, not like you, not like the others."

Oh god, oh god…he's completely insane.

My eyes flickered to the door and he noticed.

"Franny, please. I can prove it to you, but you're going to have to trust me. You're in this now, and there is nothing I can do to stop that from happening. I'm sorry if this scares you."

He lifted the shard of glass, and before I had time to scream, shoved it in his throat. Jamie dropped his hand and blood squirted out of the dark, gaping wound. His eyes rolled back and his body slumped to the floor. I ran to him, my knees hitting the floor, pressing my shaking hands against his throat. I heard a loud pitched whining noise, and it took me a moment to realize it was me screaming.

Blood poured across the wood; my knees were coated with it. His chest stopped moving and I realized he wasn't breathing. Removing my hands from his neck, I leaned back on my heels, screaming and sobbing. At some point I stood and raced to the bathroom. Naked and covered in blood, I began to vomit violently. I don't know how long I sat there, head hung in the toilet, but after some time passed, I heard a noise and looked up.

Jamie was standing in the entryway of the bathroom, alive and well. All I remember after that was blackness.

It was after sunrise when I woke up. Rolling over, I glanced at the alarm clock on the nightstand, the hands signaling it was nine in the morning. Stretching, I felt sore from top to bottom. Languidly, my eyes began to slip shut when the events of the previous night came back to me. I jumped out of the bed, scanning the room frantically for Jamie, but it was empty. There was no blood on the floor, no glass, but the dresser mirror stood empty and the room smelled like bleach. On a chair beside the bed I saw my bag. I ran over to it, meaning to grab the first thing I saw and escape through the window, when I found the note sitting on top.

Franny,
I had to go to the diner this morning. Please stay. I promise to explain everything. I will understand if you need some time, but please don't take more than a few days. We need to talk about this, and soon.
Jamie.

I shoved the note in my bag and threw on a dress, not caring if I was wearing a bra or panties. Finding my heels, I raced out the door with no intention of ever returning.

###

The morning was cool, the brisk air helping me clear my mind. At that moment, I didn't know what was real and what wasn't. Was it possible I fell asleep after sex? That it had only been a nightmare?

Yes, but that doesn't explain the mirror or the note.

If it wasn't a dream, I had to deal with the fact that I'd watched Jamie kill himself and then come back to life. I shivered.

His words came back to me.

I'm not human....We mate for life.... Now you're mine....

Pure terror filled me at the memory. I was thankful the hotel room was empty when I got there. Rebekah had left me a note, letting me know they were going to get breakfast and then catch a movie at the cinema. I set the note down and latched the door. Grabbing some clothes, I headed to the bathroom to shower. I was halfway through washing my hair when I noticed the blood under my nails. Sliding down the back of the shower, I curled into a ball and began to cry.

When my friends came back, I pretended to be too exhausted to do anything that day. Truth was, I was afraid to leave the hotel, afraid of Jamie. At the same time, I was heartbroken. I still wanted him, ached for him to comfort me…that was the scariest part of all. Rebekah was too into her new relationship with Carol to notice how odd I was acting, but Bobbie kept giving me strange looks throughout the night.

Around eight there was a knock on my door and Bobbie walked in, carrying a vase full of roses and baby's breath.

"These came for you."

I think she must have seen the fear on my face, because she put them down on the far side of the room and came to the end of my bed.

"What's wrong?"

"Nothing. I'm just tired."

"I don't believe that," she said, patting my hand. "Franny, a girl doesn't stalk a guy for a week, go spend the night with him, and then not go back to them the next day unless something went wrong."

I sighed. She was right. I was going to have to make up some excuse. Oddly enough, it never crossed my mind to tell any of them the truth.

"Honestly, I don't know what to do. I like Jamie, I really do, but he's different. He's so intense. I just don't know if I want to be a part of that."

"I understand. Did you tell him that?"

I shook my head, admitting, "No, but I think he knows."

Bobbie nodded towards the flowers. "I'm not so sure."

Jeanette started yelling Bobbie's name from the living area.

"Hey, I better go before she hunts me down. You sure you don't want to go out tonight?" she asked.

"I'm sure."

She patted my hand before leaving me alone with my thoughts. When I was sure everyone had left, I got up and looked at the floral arrangement. Tucked inside was an envelope. I pulled it open and read the inscription.

We need to talk. I'm taking tomorrow off. Meet me at my house at eight in the morning. I really miss you, Franny.

I tore the note up and flushed the pieces down the toilet. As much as it broke my heart, I never planned on seeing Jamie again. Of course, that was before the sickness started.

The next morning I awoke with an empty ache in my chest and an undeniable longing to see him. For a few seconds the pain was so intense I pulled my knees to my chest, crying in agony. After it passed, I wiped at my eyes and got dressed. Seeing my reflection in the mirror, I applied extra makeup, working hard to hide the circles under my red-rimmed eyes and pale face. I wasn't successful, because both Jeanette and Rebekah commented on it, asking me if I was getting sick. I told them I thought I was coming down with a touch of something. It wasn't entirely a lie. I really wasn't feeling well.

We had breakfast on the pier and then took a guided boat tour. Throughout the day I began to feel worse. A small pang in my stomach became full blown nausea. There was a ringing in my ears and I began to feel dizzy. They ordered pizza, and I'd just started to eat it when the sickness hit full-fledged. I ran to the bathroom, vomiting and shaking. Bobbie knocked on the door, asking if I was okay, and I yelled back, saying I thought I might have food poisoning.

Within the hour I realized the sickness had nothing to do with food, nor the flu (which I had started to suspect), but everything to do with Jamie. With a wet rag across my forehead and eyes closed, I heard his voice in my head.

Franny, I need you to come to me. This will just get worse the longer you stay away.

No....

I sent the thought back through blinding illness and nausea, not caring if the voice was real or imagined.

I heard his voice one more time.

I'm coming.

Colors began to swirl behind my eyes, shifting into places I had never been. A mountain, surrounded by forests. A lake. The images shifted again and I saw the street sign for the road we were staying on. Shops rushed by in a blur.

Everything began to spin together, taking me with it. My body was hot, skin burning with fever, but I didn't have the strength to yell for help. Suddenly there was a loud banging noise, followed by a voice.

It was Rebekah's. She was knocking. I tried to call to her but my throat was dry. I sat up, using strength I didn't know I had. The door opened and Rebekah stepped in, a look of concern on her face.

Before I had time to tell her I was dying, she said, "Jamie's here."

He stepped into the room, and the moment he did, every bit of my illness — the nausea, the fever, the visions, all of it — disappeared.

Rebekah stepped out of the room, leaving me alone with Jamie, shutting the door behind her. I was still reeling from the sudden offset of my illness, and didn't have time for the fear to set in. Picking my rag up, I stared at it in shock, unsure whether I'd dreamed the illness. The side of the bed lowered as Jamie sat beside me. I became aware of his scent, an odd, sweet musty flavor that drew me in.

When he spoke, his voice was wistful, full of emotion. "I'm sorry. I didn't realize this would happen so soon. It takes longer with my kind." Brushing the hair out of my face, he grazed his fingers under my chin and lifted it until my eyes met his. "I should have been here sooner, should have at least checked in to make sure.

Are you okay?"

Still in shock, I mumbled, "Yes."

He gave me a gentle smile and caressed my cheek. "I won't let it happen to you again, I promise. You're mine now, and I will take care of you."

The words sent shivers down my spine. He was a monster, something evil, and yet when I stared into his eyes, I was unsure of what to do.

A monster?

Maybe.

Evil?

I shook my head. Evil things don't love, and I didn't think I was mistaken when I saw compassion barely restrained behind his irises.

He waited for me to finish my thoughts. The strangest part was he seemed to know when I was done, when I was ready to talk.

"Franny, I want to talk to you, to tell you everything, but I would rather not do it here. Will you come home with me?"

"Do I have a choice?"

The words, full of venom, rolled out of my

mouth before I had the chance to stop them.

He flinched, hurt, but then shook his head. "Not really. Not if you don't want to get sick again."

I stood up curtly, a little wobbly. He reached out to steady me but I brushed him off. "Let's go."

Without a word he stood, but instead of going towards the door, he picked up my overnight bag and began packing clothes and accessories. It occurred to me that I should protest, but if he meant what he'd said, what good would it do? As I watched him pack, the reality of my new life began to kick in. I was trapped, trapped by this…man? I hated him and loved him at the same time. The thought overwhelmed me.

Dear god, I can't love him.

I felt the tears roll down my face, but didn't wipe them away.

What's the point?

Jamie spun around and looked at me. He dropped the bag on the bed and sat down beside it, hiding his face in his hands. This was not a turn I'd expected.

I had every right to be upset. Getting angry would do me no good, though. We were in this together, and there was no changing that. Quietly, I stepped over a pile of laundry and sat beside him.

Speaking softly, I told him, "I can't say I'm okay with this right now. I'm scared and I'm confused, but willing to hear you out, willing to try."

I couldn't give him any more comfort than that. I wasn't ready. He didn't look up, his hands still covering his face, so I picked up my bag and finished packing. Eventually he sat up, watching me as I grabbed the last few items and stood at the door. Slowly he stood and joined me. Taking a deep breath and placing a fake smile on my face, I cupped my hand around his and said goodbye to my friends.

Walking down the street holding Jamie's hand, I'd never been more conflicted in my life.

Two days ago I'd wished for this. Now all I wanted to do was run and never look back. But even the thought of leaving made my stomach churn. Jamie removed his hand from mine, placing an arm around my waist to steady me. Did he know how I felt, that I was thinking of running? Glancing from beneath my eyelashes, I saw the mask of misery on his face.

Yeah, he knows.

I swallowed guiltily, wondering how much he knew. Could he read my mind? Was it because we were...mated? Did it work both ways? I remembered the visions I'd had while sick. I'd known he was coming, I'd seen inside his head.

Can I do that now?

Closing my eyes, letting his arm steer me, I pulled up an image of his face, tried reaching inside his mind. At first I felt nothing, except foolish.

After a moment, I got a bleary image of the tree line in the distance. It was like looking through an obscure periscope. Colors swirled, red, then blue, making the image nearly impossible to focus on. Then I realized I could *feel* the colors. When I focused on the blue, I was overwhelmed with sadness, black brought me to anger, red, guilt. There were more red swirls than black, which made me relax a bit.

I reached out, grabbing hold of the largest swirl of color, which was purple. The scene whooshed away and overwhelmed with emotion, I fell to my knees. Jamie, surprised by my tumble, didn't catch me before the stones took off a good portion of the skin on my knees and palms.

"Are you okay?"

There was a note of panic in his voice as he helped me roll over. I leaned back on my hands, ignoring the pain, my mouth hanging open, staring at his face in disbelief.

Briefly, I felt a soft pressure in my head and knew it was him, feeling for what had me so shocked. His eyes widened and a soft "Oh" noise escaped from between his lips. He broke my gaze, becoming pallid. Instead of looking at me again, he pulled a handkerchief out of his back pocket and proceeded to gently dab the blood off my scraped knees.

He asked in a barely controlled voice, "Do you want me to carry you the rest of the way?"

With his chin hung low, he reminded me of a child preparing for their next punishment.

"Yes, I would like that."

He lifted his head, looking surprised, but then placed his arms under me, lifting me against his chest. Curious, I laid my head against it. As much as I hate to admit it, I was checking for a heartbeat. Jamie had one; it was stronger and faster than any I had heard, but it was there.

I think that was the moment I realized leaving wasn't an option for me. Even if it was, I wouldn't have left. I was going to stay with him, give up my entire life, my entire future, for this man, all because of the color purple. A color that, to this day, still means love.

Things got awkward when we arrived at

his house. I could tell that Jamie wasn't used to entertaining a guest, and had no social skills. I stood in his living room, bag in hand, for a minute while he just stared. Then he shook his head as if waking up from a dream.

"Um…. You can put your stuff in there."

He pointed to the bedroom I had escaped the day before. Walking slowly, I took the time to look around. Other than books and a few small knickknacks here and there, I had no idea what his likes or dislikes might be.

As I made my rounds, he seemed to come into some manners and asked, "Um…do you need food or a drink or anything?"

My stomach was still churning from earlier, so I shook my head. "No food." I stopped looking around his house, giving him my full attention, and asked, "Do you have any alcohol?"

Jamie looked unsure at first, but then nodded, making his way to the kitchen. I followed, opening cabinets and digging through drawers. For a cook, he had very little in the way of food. He brought a bottle of whiskey and two short glasses down from the shelf, setting them on the table.

I nodded towards the glasses. "Do you drink?"

I didn't mean it in the casual sense. I literally meant, *does your kind drink*? Although I'd seen him do it the first night, I could no longer trust it wasn't a ploy. He nodded, understanding what I meant.

I came over and poured us two glasses, half-full. I handed his glass to him and lifted mine in salute. Clinking them together, I said, "To us."

I managed to keep about half the sarcasm out of my voice. He looked at me wearily as I tilted the glass, draining its contents. He was still staring when I set the glass down. It occurred to me that this might be the quietest relationship of all time. Then I got the giggles.

I was probably still in shock from everything. At the time, though, my life suddenly seemed absolutely fucking hilarious. I couldn't stop laughing, and Jamie, poor Jamie, stood there with a look of bewilderment on his face.

I pointed at him, then to myself.

"You...," I choked on laughter, "and...me. Oh my god."

There were no more words. In truth, I had no idea what I meant by the statement, but it only made me laugh harder. I watched Jamie struggle with his emotions...confusion, then anger. I briefly worried he might kill me, and that sent me into another fit of hysterical laughter. Then, out of the blue, he began to laugh along with me.

We sat in that kitchen, both of us, laughing until tears streamed down our faces. Every time one of us would start to calm down, the other one would just start laughing harder. When there was more silence than laughter, I poured myself another drink and leaned back in the chair.

As crazy and senseless as it was, we'd just had our first real moment together. Jamie took a sip of his drink and cleared his throat, speaking with a flourish I had never imagined he was capable of.

"I wasn't born this way," he said, pointing to his chest. "Not in this body, but for the most part it's all I remember. Our kinds were nomadic, hunted by humans, but their anger at us was not undeserved. We don't have...." He furrowed his brow, struggling for the words. "A conscience like your kind. Food is food, hunting is hunting. We would attack and kill our own families if the need arose."

He took a sip of his drink before continuing.

"My family was no different. We were staying close to a village, hunting down farm animals, the occasional hunter too, when my brother went too far and attacked a priest in plain daylight. I was maybe six months old. There are very few ways we can die, but the people of that town figured one of them out. They hunted us down mercilessly, killing us one at a time until only my mother—seriously injured—and I were left. We stumbled upon a house where a young mother had just given birth. It was an old magic my mother used, one not used by any of us in a long time, and she was weak, but succeeded for the most part. She replaced the human child with me and left. I never saw her again."

The longing in his voice made me want to comfort him, but at that moment, I don't think he even remembered I was there. I waited, enraptured, for him to continue. When he finally did, it wasn't without some trepidation.

"My mother—my human mother—she knew something was wrong with me, that I was different. At times I would hear her crying in the corner, and once I heard her tell a priest I wasn't her child, that I was an evil thing. But she loved me the best she could. In most part, I think it was because she was so lonely. My father was never home, and she tended the homestead by herself. On the other hand, I also think it's because there was still a little bit of her son left in me too. Like I said, my real mother was weak when she used the old magic. Not all of the human side was purged.

"I loved her, in a way. At least, I tried. After a while, I started realizing what human behavior was acceptable and what was not. I did my best to abide by these...these *rules,*" he said, frowning as if the word disgusted him. "When I failed, my mother would cover for me, hide the evidence. Still, people talked. When my father would come home for a stint, he would hear the rumors and beat me. Twice he beat me to death, only to find me breathing a few minutes later. As I grew, I think he became scared of me, so he started beating my mom instead. I was sixteen when I heard her screams from across the field. I ran to the house, ax in tow, to find my father standing over my mother, her head bashed in with the log he had been beating her with. He glared at me, his eyes feverish, and said, 'This is your fault, you evil bastard.' I dropped my ax and killed him with my bare hands, relishing the sounds of his screams."

A grin broke across his face, and I saw a glimpse of the creature inside of him. His reverie broke and he remembered I was there. "I'm sorry. I'm scaring you. aren't I?" I struggled for the lie, but he interrupted me. "I can smell the fear on you."

That phrase from anyone would have been enough to make me cringe. From Jamie, it was absolutely paralyzing.

Purple... purple means love. Remember that.

"I won't hurt you, Franny," he said in a matter-of-fact tone.

I think I nodded — maybe I just stared — but he continued anyway.

"I traveled after that, working places here and there. That's one thing my human mother instilled in me, the ability to cook. I remember her saying that no matter what, there was always the need for a good cook. I've tried to track down others of my type, but I've only come across dead ends and rumors, which led me here, to you."

"Did you come searching for your kind? Are there more here?" The thought terrified and intrigued me at the same time.

"No." He set down his drink. "I came here

for solitude. After all my searches, I think I might be the last one left."

The silence stretched, and I knew he was waiting for me to ask the question, but I hesitated, afraid of the answer. Finally he stood, picking up his chair and setting it down beside me.

"Franny, you can ask me anything and I won't lie to you. We're bound to each other now."

I took a deep breath and asked, "What are you?"

"Technically, I'm a changeling, or at least according to folklore. That's what I've heard them call creatures who are switched with a human child."

"And what were you before that?"

"Our kind called ourselves rakbanes. We are older than your kind, but by the time the human population began to grow, most of us were gone. We do not breed very often. Maybe one child is born to each family every century, so we began to die out very quickly. You can see why I think I might be the last."

"What do…rakbanes look like?"

"To your eyes, we would look like demons. That's part of the reason we were hunted so much. In truth, we have no religious affiliation. We are simply instinctual creatures, a part of this earth, no more, no less." He leaned over and grabbed my hand, putting it on his face and saying, "This is what *I* look like though."

Touching his face, I felt the attraction swell in my stomach again, but my mind fought it off. As much as Jamie knew, he had missed one important detail…humans could be instinctual too. We just had a better control of ours. I removed my hand from his face, the questions racing through my mind.

"If you didn't grow up with your parents, how do you know all this? And you said there was a little of Jamie left in you. What did that mean?"

"We are born with the knowledge, at least to some extent. My mother was weak, the magic old, and some of Jamie was left inside.

Sometimes, though, I wonder if she did it on purpose. If she thought leaving a little human in me would give me a better chance at life. Remember how I said that when I first saw you, I was drawn to you?"

I nodded.

"Well, I thought you might be a changeling, like me, but you weren't. I think it was the Jamie part of me that was drawn to you."

The alcohol began to take hold, but I poured one more glass anyway, telling myself it could have been worse. He could have been a demon from hell or some type of flesh-eating monster.

"What does this mean for me?"

He sighed and sat back in his chair. I didn't have to intrude into his head to see the conflicting emotions.

"It means, whether or not you want it, you're stuck with me. When we mate, we mate for life. Our seed contains an element that alters the other's chemistry, binding us together. We will always know where the other is, how they are feeling, if they are sick. On the other hand, being away from your mate too long will cause illness and finally death, for both. One cannot live without the other."

"Oh, god…."

"I'm sorry, Franny, I really am."

"Does that mean…am I like you now?"

"No," he said, sitting up abruptly. "I mean, I don't think so."

"You don't know?"

Jamie stood, pacing the kitchen, pulling at his hair. "There's no knowledge of what happens if we mate with one of your kind. I don't think it's ever been done. It surprised me how quickly the illness took root in you, and it surprised me even more that you could get inside my head." At that acknowledgment, his eyes flickered towards me. "You know how I feel now, what you mean to me. It's not something I can change or control. All I can promise to do is protect you the best I can, from the world…and from myself."

"Do I need protection from you?"

He hung his head. "Yes, you might."

Oddly enough, I didn't think I would. I already trusted him. Was that instinctual, too? I stood and walked over to him. "Thank you for being honest with me, Jamie. I need some time to think about this, to sleep on it."

"Of course. You'll stay, right? I can sleep on the couch."

"Do I have a choice?"

He shook his head.

The night held very little sleep for me. No matter how many times I tried to shut the thoughts out, I would find myself reviewing our conversation a few minutes later. After three hours of doing this, tossing and turning, I came to one final thought…none of it mattered. I could overthink it, be fearful of the future, but what good would it do? I was stuck with him, for better or worse, sickness and health. That left one option; try to be happy with what I had.

We were going to have to come up with a plan, maybe an elopement. I also realized I was going to have to trust my instincts when it came to how I felt about him. So far he had been nothing but open and honest with me. At least that's what I thought. It would be many years down the road before I realized he'd lied to me about something very important.

When I was seven, another kid at my school, an overweight freckled boy, spent a week teasing me relentlessly about my mousy hair and pointy nose...both features I would grow into as an adult, but to a seven-year-old child, it was torture. I complained to my parents all week, both taking turns trying to console my hurt ego. By the end of the week, I demanded my mother talk to his parents. I was surprised when she gave me a stern no. I yelled at her for the first time in my memory, accusing her of being too afraid to talk to his parents, of not loving me, and then I ran to my room and slammed the door. She came to the door shortly after, knocking before entering and sitting beside me on the bed. I hugged my pillow, soaked with tears, to my chest while she spoke.

"Franny, here's the thing; I could go talk to his parents and they would go home and punish him, maybe even make him apologize. Then, when the next person says something bad about you, and it will happen, you'll want me to do the same. The point is, there is always going to be a bully, bad things are going to happen to you, and sometimes you're not going to like the situation you're in. When those times come, you can't always expect someone to come along and make things better. Sometimes you've just got to stand up, shake the dust off, and do the best you can with what you have."

It was with that thought in my head I made my way to the kitchen the next morning. Jamie, wearing only sweats, was standing in front of the stove, cooking breakfast.

I could do worse; he's not hard to look at.

"Good morning."

He cautiously returned the greeting, but I felt him in my head again, tasting my emotions all the same. I let him do it, but planned to put a stop to it soon. Jamie must have liked what he found because he smiled. I sat at the table as he finished cooking, realizing it was past nine in the morning.

"Aren't you supposed to be at work?" I asked.

He put the food on the plates and sat across from me. "I took the day off."

"Oh," I said, looking down at the pile of crepes.

Jamie ran his hands through his hair. "I... um...I didn't know what else you liked to eat."

"No, these are great," I said, picking up the fork, trying not to laugh.

We were practically strangers, an issue we needed to correct.

"So, I was thinking that we need to come up with a plan this morning, a story we can tell my friends and family to explain why we are spending so much time together."

Did I imagine it, or did he suddenly look hopeful?

"Then, this afternoon, I think we should

spend some time getting to know each other."

No, I didn't imagine it.

"I'd like that, a lot," he said, smiling genuinely.

We spent the morning throwing ideas around, but it all came back to the same thing… we needed to get married. How odd it was to discuss our marriage plan as if it were nothing more than the dinner menu for the week. My dreams of a beautiful white wedding gown, all eyes on me, were so easily brushed off to the side. Maybe he saw the longing in my eyes, or maybe he peeked inside my head, but he quickly revised the idea.

"How about we say we've fallen madly in love and get engaged? Then we can have a proper wedding."

I agreed, already dreading the phone call to my parents where I tried to explain this whirlwind romance. Still, it was better than his initial idea, which was to have me become the next missing person. I was surprised to find out, when I worried about money, that Jamie had quite a lot of it. But I was too afraid to ask him how he'd come in to that kind of money.

After the difficult decisions were made, Jamie stood up and took me by the hand, saying, "Come on, I want to show you something."

We passed by the bedroom into a door I hadn't realized was there. Inside was a small room, easels and paint spread out across a white table. Hung all over the walls were paintings, dozens of them. Three depicted me. In one I was sitting at the café. Two were profiles. Looking at them, I felt beautiful.

"You did all these?" The awe in my voice was an understatement to how I felt.

"Yes. You wanted to know about me. This is me." He pointed to a picture of a lady, her dark hair braided, staring out the window. "That was my human mother."

I walked up to the picture, taking in her plain face. There was pain etched in, but also compassion. My heart went out to the woman who'd fought to protect her un-human child.

Beneath the frame, sitting on the floor, was

a collection of canvases, facing backward. I reached to pick one up but Jamie grabbed my wrist. I instantly knew what was painted on the other canvases, what he wouldn't want me to see. I nodded to his hand, pleading with my eyes. I had to know. Slowly he released me and took a few steps back. I flipped the first canvas over.

The creature that stared back at me was pale, with whitish-gray scaled skin and obsidian eyes. It was humanoid and elongated, but hunched over. There was no hair or eyelashes, no ears, only two dark slits where a nose should be. Maybe it was because of the situation I was in, but I thought I saw a sadness in the creature. I took a deep breath, testing my own emotions, surprised at what I found.

I'm okay with this.

"Your mother?" I asked, not looking at him.

"Yes."

Because of the pale skin and the dark background, I asked, "Nocturnal?"

"Yes."

I didn't have to ask why. Besides being easier to hunt at night, it would have kept them safer from being hunted.

"Are you?"

"No, I've adapted."

I remembered our conversation about the dark, where he said that people were different in the dark.

"Is that why you didn't want to be around me at night?"

"It's harder for me to...resist my nature when it is dark."

"Oh."

I'd found myself saying that a lot lately. Then again, what else was there to say? I picked the painting up and set it on the counter, below his human mother, and turned to face Jamie. He was watchful of my every move, cautious, but I wasn't going to balk or run.

I took his hand and asked, "What else do you have to show me?"

We spent the rest of the day talking about things we liked, our lives. I found out Jamie was not only an artist, but a limitless dictionary of historical knowledge, something we were both passionate about. He spent most of his days reading about history, religion, mythology. We debated, argued, and laughed. When supper time came around, he asked if it would be okay if he took me out to eat, and I said yes.

I showered and dressed in one of my finer dresses. When I stepped into the living room, his eyes widened, looking me up and down. I bit my lip and felt heat rush to my cheeks. He made me feel so beautiful.

Jamie cleaned up very well. I couldn't seem to keep my eyes off him.

We went to one of the fanciest restaurants I had ever been to in my life. I didn't know what to order so he ordered several things, explaining what they were when I tried them. He fed me dessert from his own spoon, slipping it into my mouth and watching me enjoy it. It occurred to me that he was trying to court me. Afterward, we went to the cinema and caught a movie. I couldn't focus on it because he held my hand, rubbing my palm with his thumb. He spent most of the movie staring at me, and I shyly glanced down. Tentatively I reached into his mind again, feeling the colors. There was a new color there that night, orange...desire.

I was happy when the movie was over. We walked home, hand in hand.

When we got there, he made up the couch, kissed me on the forehead, and said, "Goodnight, Franny."

I went to the room, disappointed, and began to change into my night clothes, but decided against it. I stripped down naked and walked back into the living room, standing above him.

Jamie looked at me, the desire in his eyes, but argued, "I can't trust myself not to hurt you."

"I trust you." No, that wasn't enough. I didn't want him to just have sex with me. "I want you to make love to me."

He stood, slowly running the back of his hand over my face, down to the hard points of my nipples. I understood then. It was against his nature to be gentle, a struggle for him, but he did it anyway. His lips met mine, trembling from his internal battle, soft. We broke the kiss and he lifted me like a child, carrying me to bed. He told me he loved me as he entered me.

That night, and most nights (some days) thereafter, we shared the bed together. Sometimes we made love, other times the sex was carnal, animalistic, but both pleasing in their own way.

We married in Paris, then hopped on a plane for home to tell my parents. They were leery of Jamie, understandably so, but since they only saw him a few times in the duration of their lives, it didn't matter much. I was happy, so they tried not to question it. We were three months into our married lives together when I killed him the first time.

It was the flu that did it. An epidemic was moving through Paris. Doctors' offices and hospitals were full. People walked around, their faces covered with scarves or masks. I hadn't realized Jamie could get sick. In the weeks following us being together, I learned a lot about him. He was stronger than humanly possible, could see in the dark, his eyesight ranged for miles, and although I could only see into his mind, he could see through everyone.

It started off as the sniffles, which had me laughing at him, joking about how a little cold could turn the strongest men into babies. He joked along with me until the fever and vomiting started. I tried to get him to go to the doctor but he refused, and I couldn't argue with him. Jamie was *passably* human, but a close physical might give away the truth.

"Plus, it's not like I'll die from this, Franny," he joked.

I wasn't so sure. As the fever grew stronger, he became erratic, lashing out at me when I brought him broth or water. On the second night I found him crouched in a corner, growling. I stood at the door, shaking in fear, trying to calm him. Approaching slowly, I knelt, holding my hands out. He watched warily as I closed the space between us, his body stiffening.

When I thought it was okay, I gently touched his face.

It was a trick…he was letting me feel secure. He launched at me and we flew across the room. My head hit the floor, causing my teeth to gnash together. Spots swam across my vision. He was crouched over me, growling, his eyes shining. I couldn't move, couldn't fight back. I tried to reach into his mind but failed the first few times, a vile anger pushing me back. His hands circled my throat, cutting off my air. I tried again, struggling to breathe, and succeeded. What I saw in his mind, his true nature, would forever scar me.

Jamie, please, I love you.

His face flickered, shifting from predator to lover. He released me, shoving my body far from him. I hit the dresser with my back.

"Kill me," he growled.

"No," I whimpered, shaking and crying. "I won't."

He barked out a high pitched howl that

shook the windows. Low and menacing, he screamed, "If I kill you, it will kill me. Now do it!"

"Please don't make me, Jamie."

I wailed this time, but through tears, looked around for a weapon. Above me, on the top of the dresser, was a letter opener. I grabbed it, cradling it to my chest, praying I wouldn't have to use it.

Jamie didn't give me a choice. He launched at me again, spitting and growling. I brought the letter opener up, shoving it into his throat. At first he continued growling, but then his body started swaying and he fell onto my lap. Crying, shocked, I sat there for the next hour, running my hands through his hair, saying I'm sorry repeatedly until I felt his heart start to beat again.

After that, at Jamie's insistence, I always carried a weapon.

When we talked about it later, he had no memory of what happened, but said, "I'm glad you stabbed me in the neck. Had it been the heart, I would have died."

That was the second and last lie he ever told me during our marriage.

For days afterward I shook in fear. Slowly he worked with me, helping me to cope, but there would always be a little part of my heart that broke that night.

We were married for twenty-five years before I discovered the truth.

We traveled in search of his kind. We ate and laughed, made love often. When the money ran low, Jamie would sell some paintings. Overall, things were well. I was happy, blissfully married, with the exception of occasionally having to kill my husband.

We were traveling through Ireland, enjoying the sunset from our patio, when I noticed someone standing below, eyes gleaming yellow in the moonlight, staring up at us. Jamie, acting nervously, put his arm around my waist and led me inside, making love to me until I forgot all about the man with yellow eyes. The next day I saw him watching us from a distance two more times as we checked out some shops. I mentioned it to Jamie and his eyes became slits.

"It's a wraith, baby. He's probably following us because he senses me and is curious. It's nothing to worry about, but we should avoid him nonetheless."

"What's a wraith?"

"It's an evil spirit that has possessed a body. This one is old, hateful, seeking vengeance."

I shivered, but then a thought occurred to me. "If it's old, maybe it knows about your kind. Should we talk to him?" I asked.

"No."

Jamie didn't give a reason, and I knew better than to ask. Still, the thought stuck with me. It was two days later when Jamie was off selling some paintings that I saw the wraith standing underneath the patio again. I took the stairs down, two at a time. The wraith stood in plain daylight, its yellow eyes glaring, mouth stretched into a rotten tooth filled smile.

Its voice was raspy, hollow. "You came to

me, child."

I stayed a few feet back, asking, "Why are you following my husband?"

It laughed, a scratchy sound that gave me chills. "Surely you know what he is?" I nodded, my voice temporarily lost. It stepped closer. I smelled rotten meat and garbage. "It is not your husband I am following, child, it is you. I am curious as to why you are with such a beast."

"I love him," I whispered, unable to lie in its presence. "He loves me, too."

The wraith spit, "His kind is incapable of love."

"That's not true. He does love me." Without warning, I started crying and said, "It's not like I could leave anyway."

This thing was so evil...I could feel it feeding off my emotions, but I could not turn away.

"Is that what he's told you?" the wraith asked, stepping forward. "Yes, I can see it now. So many lies. You want to know the truth, child?"

I nodded, unable to stop myself.

The creature spoke at length. "You are not trapped. His kind, they do not mate for life. They mate for children. They take their womenkind, fill them with their seed, and if they do not become pregnant, they leave them to die from the poison."

"They can't," I said, shaking my head. "You lie. They would die too."

"Another lie. Rakbanes can only be killed by their own poison or beheading. They are venomous. They died out because they killed their own kind. The venom, it weakens in their presence. As long as the one who has poisoned you stays close, the venom will wear off within a week."

"No."

My body shook as it fed off my emotions.

"Oh, yes, my child. He does bed you at least once a week, doesn't he? Fills you with his seed? Take a break for a while, turn him down, and run. See how far you can get."

"You lie!"

"Why would I lie when the truth is so delectable?" I felt him reach deeper into my thoughts, driving me to my knees. "Ah, you think he can die? If you stab him in the heart? So, romantic." He stuck a bony finger to the side of his face. "Rakbanes are shapeshifters, my dear little girl. If you stab him in the heart, you destroy the body, forcing him to shift into his own form."

The wraith came to me then, sticking a dirt-caked hand under my chin and lifting my face to his waxy one.

"I will give you this, my sweet…the creature must love you to throw a life of eternity away just to wither in this shell of a body. I have enjoyed our little talk, child. It is nice to meet the woman who tamed a rakbane."

When Jamie found me I was on the street, shivering, too weak to get up. He carried me to bed, smelling the wraith on me. At some point during the night he left, I assumed to hunt it down, but we never spoke of it again. I didn't tell Jamie what was spoken, only that I couldn't remember anything, locking the information up behind a mental wall which Jamie himself had taught me how to do.

I tried to believe everything the wraith had told me was a lie, but the doubt was there and I had to know the truth. For two weeks I avoided sex, claiming I was still recovering emotionally from the wraith's touch. By the second week Jamie became very nervous and moody. He did not force me, but there were times when I could see it in his eyes...he was thinking about it.

My break came when a gallery requested a new piece from him. I complained of a stomachache and stayed home, leaving me alone for the entire day. Shortly after he was gone, I got in the car and drove for hours. By the time I turned around I was shaking and crying, but not because I was ill. It was because he had lied. I wasn't bonded to him.

When I walked in the door and threw down the keys, he was waiting for me, cowering on the couch like a scared child. He knew I'd discovered the truth about the illness. Reaching into his mind I saw the sorrow and the heartbreak, the fear I was going to leave him. What he didn't know was that I understood why he did it. Why else would I have stayed with a creature such as himself?

I also knew the only reason he had never told me the truth was because he never had enough confidence in my love for him to do so.

Instead of trying to reassure him by telling him I understood, that I loved him, I grabbed his hand and took him to bed. When he tried to pull out instead of filling me with his seed, I pushed him in deeper. Afterward he lay on me, crying, and I held him as he shook.

I never told him that the wraith had told me he was a shapeshifter, and that he couldn't die. That secret I kept in my heart forever.

Franny doubled over, the pain spreading from her lower back into her stomach, sweat covering her brow. The cigarette dropped to the floor, its flame burning into the wood. When the pain stopped she put her foot on it, crushing the remaining ash. The cursor on the computer blinked, taunting her to finish. She twitched, knocking the empty glass to the floor as she fought for the last few minutes of her story.

Jamie, my love, I will speak directly to you now. I do not have much time left since I am not sure if I will survive this. It was after you were diagnosed with Alzheimer's that I discovered I was pregnant. My belly began to grow, life moving within me, but I knew something was unnatural about it. It was then I searched for the wraith that nearly destroyed me that day.

For weeks I thought I searched in vain, thought maybe you had destroyed him as you sought to do. I had given up hope when he came to me, sensing my distress, my need. He told me the truth about your kind, a truth not even you knew. If you had, I don't think you would have ever touched me again. I know now why your kind was so few, so small.

You see, rakbanes do not procreate, they recreate. They impregnate the females when they become old so they will have another body, a shell of themselves to shapeshift into. What I carry in me is not a child at all, but a vessel for you.

In time you will grow to know this, but by then, I suspect I will no longer be with you. I do not even know if I will survive this birth, and even if I do I have only a short time to care for you before my life comes to an end. Your body lies on the bed in the other room, a knife through your heart. I am sorry for that, for betraying you. You would have let yourself die in that body before living a life without me, before shapeshifting. Now I will do the same for you.

I will never regret the first time we met, the life we had. I love you so much. When I am gone there will be a little of me inside you, as there was a little bit of Jamie, so do not fret over the loss. We will be together for eternity.

###

As her story began to print, Franny crawled

to the bedroom, unable to walk any further, and pulled herself up in bed, beside her husband, kissing him gently on his dead lips before screaming in agony as the child began to push its way out.

Epilogue

A shrill cry pierced the night. An old mother held her newborn child, its gray, glowing eyes staring at her.

She caressed his cheek, whispering, "Jamie...."

The End

Heather Harrison has published several stories including *I, Avatar* and *To Reap and Sow*. She writes press releases for businesses to help improve their visibility. Heather also markets social media platforms and assists other authors in developing their websites, graphics, and social media outreach. When writing fiction, she primarily focuses on Young Adult, Horror, and Science Fiction/Fantasy. Heather and her two children live in Dallas, Texas.